Breathe In. Breathe Out.

By Meredith Stack

Thank you to my beautiful family. Brian, Tyson, Riley, and Dylan, I love you so much.

Thank you also to all those who helped create this book especially Kerri McCaffrey, Carter Gavlick, Mila Elms, Hadley and Stella Moores- you are the best!

As a working mom with a husband, three boys and two dogs, I juggle work, multiple schedules, meals, cleaning and laundry. Days can get pretty hectic. I find meditation to be an extremely useful tool that not only helps me stay focused but keeps me aligned with who I truly am and makes decision-making much easier.

Just recently, I noticed one of my sons was anxious about his schoolwork. He was having a hard time falling asleep at night too. I could identify with him, since I used to have that same problem. My mind would race thinking of all the things I had to do the next day. Since meditation was so helpful for me, I began introducing meditation to him as well. To my surprise, he liked it! It helped him focus on something other than the things that were worrying him. Meditation started helping him, just as it helped me.

Soon after that, I began incorporating meditation into all my boys' lives, no matter what the age. I realized that it is never too early to start the practice. The Breathe In, Breathe Out approach is a very simple way to begin the process of taking a break and breathing through your emotions. In contrast to the "time out" approach, which feels more like a punishment, this approach conveys the message that it is normal to have emotions. Getting angry, frustrated or nervous are all normal experiences, but how we deal with those emotions is important. By stepping away and concentrating on your breath, you can increase oxygen to your brain while stimulating your nervous system to create a sense of calm. Then you can address the issue much more mindfully.

This book covers the first step in introducing the concept of meditation. It is easy to follow, understand and remember. I recommend you read it to your child in advance and then reread it when a stressful time actually occurs. Once he/she understands the concept, you may leave the book for your child in his/her "special place," and he/she can begin to turn to it when stressful situations arise. You may also ask them to repeat the two main phrases from the book, "Breathe In. Breathe Out. That's what it's all about," and "Breathe In. Breath Out. This will pass I have no doubt." These phrases can serve as mantras that the child can use to help calm his- or herself down, wherever they may be.

Another suggestion, which I especially love, is what we call "My Mantra Monkey." I bought a stuffed animal monkey for each one of my children, and when they are having a hard time with something, I bring out their special Mantra Monkey to hold while they sit and breathe. We pick a mantra for that moment, like, "This will pass I have no doubt," "Breathe In, Breath Out" or "All is Okay." and repeat the phrase as we close our eyes and hug our monkey. Mantra Monkey is always a good friend to have when things are just not going your way.

Good luck, and if you have any questions please visit www.meredithstack.com, or email me. Now go start meditating!

Breathe in. Breathe Out.
That's what this is all about.

When I get mad, when I want to roar.
I cross my legs, I sit on the floor.

Breathe In. Breathe Out.
This will pass I have no doubt.

When I can't do this and I can't do that.
I want to scream, I want to pout.

Breathe In. Breathe Out.
I decide, I will not shout.

When he makes me mad or pulls
my hair.
I want to yell, "It's just not fair!"

Breathe In. Breathe Out.
This will pass, I have no doubt.

I move away, I sit and stay.
I take my break, then return to play.

Breathe In. Breathe Out.
That's what this is all about.

These feelings will pass, I know they will.

I close my eyes, I get real still.

Breathe in. Breathe Out.
It's passing now, I have no doubt.

With each breath, I release my fears.
I'm OK now. I can wipe my tears.

Breathe In. Breathe Out.
I did it!
I never had, a breath of doubt!

CPSIA information can be obtained
at www.ICGtesting.com
Printed in the USA
LVOW05s0315180717
541738LV00008B/15/P